Presented to

_____

by _____

on _____

LULLABIES
for little hearts

Songs by Carol Smith
Illustrated by Elena Kucharik

**TYNDALE
KIDS**

Tyndale House Publishers, Inc.
WHEATON, ILLINOIS

Visit Tyndale's exciting Web site at www.tyndale.com

OTHER BOOKS IN THE LITTLE BLESSINGS LINE:
Bibles for Little Hearts *compiled by The Livingstone Corporation*
Bible for Little Hearts
Prayers for Little Hearts
Promises for Little Hearts
Questions from Little Hearts *by Kathleen Long Bostrom*
What Is God Like?
Who Is Jesus?

Lyrics and music written by Carol Smith.
Designed by Catherine Bergstrom

Developed for Tyndale House Publishers, Inc., by The Livingstone Corporation.

Printed in Singapore

07 06 05 04 03 02 01 00 99
10 9 8 7 6 5 4 3 2 1

Lie Down in Peace

Psalm 4:8

You can lie down in peace.
You can lie down and sleep.
God will keep you safe.

You can lie down in peace.
You can lie down and sleep.
God will keep you safe.

CHORUS:

Safe in your bed, safe in his arms—
You will be safe till morning comes.
Safe in your bed, safe in his arms—
You will be safe till morning comes.

2

Close your eyes now in peace.
Close your eyes now and sleep.
God will keep you safe.

Close your eyes now in peace.
Close your eyes now and sleep.
God will keep you safe.

CHORUS

You can dream now in peace.
You can dream now and sleep.
God will keep you safe.

You can dream now in peace.
You can dream now and sleep.
God will keep you safe.

CHORUS

Watching Over You

Psalm 3:5

CHORUS:

God is watching you,
Watching over you.
God is watching you,
Watching over you.

REPEAT CHORUS

9

When you close your eyes at night,
God is watching over you.
Till you see the morning light,
God is watching over you.
You can see the stars and moon.
But the sun will come up soon.
And . . .

CHORUS:

God is watching you,
Watching over you.
God is watching you,
Watching over you.

11

When you fall asleep in bed,
God is watching over you.
When your last good-night is said,
God is watching over you.
Pull the covers to your chin
Till the day can start again.
And . . .

CHORUS:

God is watching you,
Watching over you.
God is watching you,
Watching over you.

God is watching over you
All night long.
God is watching over you
All night long.

All night long,
All night long,
God is watching over you
All night long.

14

Go to sleep, my little one;
God is watching over you.
Till you see the morning sun,
God is watching over you.
You're as safe as you can be.
And come morning you will see
That . . .

CHORUS:

God is watching you,
Watching over you.
God is watching you,
Watching over you.

REPEAT CHORUS

Like a Shepherd

Isaiah 40:11

A shepherd feeds his little lambs;
He gives them food to eat.
A shepherd feeds his little lambs;
He gives them what they need.

A shepherd is the one who
Watches over those he loves.
God is like a shepherd, too,
Watching us from up above.
You are his little lamb.
You are his little lamb.

REPEAT THE LAST TWO LINES

A shepherd holds his little lambs
Safely in his arms.
A shepherd holds his little lambs
Right beside his heart.

CHORUS

20

A shepherd leads his little lambs
And leads the mother sheep.
A shepherd leads his little lambs
So they can safely sleep.

CHORUS

23

Right by Your Side
Hebrews 13:5-6

There's never a minute
That God isn't in it.
There's never a second
He's not on your side.
There isn't an hour
That he would not help you,
Not one speck of daylight
That he lets slip by.

Even a whisper—
God still can hear it.
He hears all your laughter;
He sees all your tears,
'Cause he's always listening,
And he always cares.
So don't be afraid;
God is with you here.

Right by your side—
He's right by your side.
Right by your side—
He's right by your side.

There's never a minute
When God cannot see you.
There's never a second
When he turns away.
There isn't an hour
When he doesn't love you,
Not one speck of nighttime
That he doesn't stay.

CHORUS

God Always Listens

Psalm 120:1

You might whisper by your bedside,
Telling God about your day.
You can speak so quietly
That no one else will hear.
But God hears, and he'll answer
your prayer.

You might cry into your pillow
Or start laughing right out loud.
No matter what you say,
No matter when, no matter where,
God hears, and he'll answer
your prayer.

God always listens.
He will be there.
He'll somehow answer
Each one of your prayers.

You might swing out on the playground,
Asking God to help your friend.
You might speak out loud, and no one
Hears you anywhere.
But God hears, and he'll answer
your prayer.

You might feel a little sad,
And you might need God's help
to smile.
You may be alone,
And it seems like nobody cares.
But God cares, and he'll answer
your prayer.

CHORUS

God Pours His Love

Psalm 42:8

Through each day God pours
his love upon us
Like the rain falls from the sky.

Through each night we sing his songs
Because he gives us life.

That's why we pray; that's how we know
That he is with us wherever we go.
That's why we pray—we know he's near.
We know that God is with us here.

God Cares

I Peter 5:7

Are you worried about something—
Maybe one thing, maybe two?
When you're worried or
you're scared,
God cares what's happening to you.

Are you feeling something's wrong,
And you don't know what to do?
When you're nervous or afraid,
God cares what's happening to you.

CHORUS:

You can give him all your fears.
You can let him keep them.
You can give him all your tears.
You can go to sleep then.

52

Is it time to go to bed
Even though there's lots to do?
When it's hard to lie so still,
God cares what's happening to you.

CHORUS

Your Room's Filled with Love

James 4:8

When you know God's near you,
When you know he's here,
You know your room's filled
with love.
When you can remember
That God never leaves you,
You know your room's filled
with love.

CHORUS:

God never goes away from you.
He promised he'd always stay.
But you might forget he's here, and then
He'll seem so far away.

If you close your eyes

And imagine your room
Wrapped around you like a hug—
If you close your eyes
And remember God's with you,
You'll know your room's filled
with love.

CHORUS:

God never goes away from you.
He promised he'd always stay.
But you might forget he's here,
and then
He'll seem so far away.

God never leaves.
He never leaves;
He never leaves.
He's right here with you.
That's where he'll
always stay.

Lie Down in Peace

Psalm 4:8—I will lie down in peace and sleep, for you alone, O Lord, will keep me safe.

You can lie down in peace.___ You can

lie down and sleep.__ God will keep you safe. You can

lie down in peace.__ You can lie down and sleep.___

God will keep you ___ safe. Safe in your bed. ___

Safe in his arms. ___ You will be safe Till morn-ing comes.___

Safe in your bed, ___ Safe in his arms.___

You will be safe___ Till morn - ing comes.___

Watching Over You

Psalm 3:5—I lay down and slept. I woke up in safety,
for the Lord was watching over me.

God is watch - ing you, watch-ing o - ver you._____

God is watch - ing you, watch-ing o - ver you._____

When you close your eyes_____ at night,___God is

watch-ing ov - er you. When you see the morn - ing light,__God is

watch-ing ov - er you. You can see the stars____and moon. But the

sun will come_____up soon. And God is watch - ing you,

watch-ing o - ver you._____When you fall a - sleep in bed, God is

watch-ing o - ver you. When your last good-night is said, God is watch-ing ov - er you. Pull the cov - ers to your chin, Till the day can start a - gain, And God is watch - ing you, watch-ing o - ver you._____ God is watch - ing you, watch-ing o - ver you._____ God is watch - ing o - ver you,___ All night long. God is watch - ing o - ver you,___ All night long. All night long, All night long, God is watch - ing o - ver you,___ All night long.

Like a Shepherd

Isaiah 40:11—He will feed his flock like a shepherd. He will carry the lambs in his arms, holding them close to his heart. He will gently lead the mother sheep with their young.

A shep-herd feeds his lit - tle lambs; He

gives them food to eat. A shep-herd feeds his lit - tle lambs; He

gives them what they need. A shep - herd is the one who

watch-es ov - er those he loves. God is like a shep-herd too,

Watch-ing us from up a - bove. You are his lit - tle___ lamb.___

_____ You are his lit - tle lamb._____

You are his lit - tle___ lamb. You are his lit - tle lamb.

Right by Your Side

Hebrews 13:5-6—*God has said, "I will never fail you. I will never forsake you." That is why we can say with confidence, "The Lord is my helper, so I will not be afraid."*

There's nev-er a min-ute that God is-n't in it. There's nev-er a sec-ond he's not on your side. There is-n't an ho-ur that he would not help you, Not one speck of day-light that he lets slip by. Ev-en a whis-per— God still can hear it. He hears all your laugh-ter; he sees all your tears, 'Cause he's al-ways listen-ing, and he al-ways cares. So don't be a-fraid; God is with you here.

Right by your side,_____ He's right

by your side._____ Right by your side,

He's right by your side.___ Ev - en a whis - per—

God still can hear it. He hears all your laugh-ter; He

sees all your tears, 'Cause he's al - ways listen - ing, and

he al - ways cares. So don't be a - fraid, God is

with you here. Right by your side_____

He's right by your side_____ Right

by your side, He's right by your side._____

God Always Listens

*Psalm 120:1—I took my troubles to the Lord; I cried
out to him, and he answered my prayer.*

You might whis - per by your bed - side,

Tel - ling God a - bout your day.

You can speak so qui - et - ly that

no one else will hear._____ But

God hears, and he'll an - swer your prayer.

You might cry in - to your pil - low

Or start laugh - ing right out loud. No

mat - ter   what   you   say,   no   mat - ter

when,   no   mat - ter   where,——

God   hears, and   he'll   an - swer your   prayer.

God   al - ways   list - ens._____

He   will   be   there._____

He'll   some - how   an - swer   Each

one   of   your   prayers._____   Each

one   of   your   prayers._____

God Pours His Love

Psalm 42:8—Through each day the Lord pours his unfailing love upon me, and through each night I sing his songs, praying to God who gives me life.

Through each day God pours his love up-on us Like the rain falls from the sky. Through each night we sing his songs Be-cause he gives us life. That's why____ we pray; That's how we know That he____ is with us wher-ev-er we go. That's why____ we pray— We know____ he's near. We know____ that God is with us here._____

72

God Cares

I Peter 5:7—Give all your worries and cares to God, for he cares about what happens to you.

Are you wor - ried a - bout some-thing— May - be one thing, may - be two? When you're wor - ried or you're scared, God cares what's hap - pen - ing to you.

Are you feel - ing some - thing's wrong, And you don't know what to do? When you're ner - vous or a - fraid, God cares what's hap - pen - ing to you.

You can give him all your fears. You can let him keep them. You can give him all your tears. You can go to sleep then.

Your Room's Filled with Love

James 4:8—Come near to God and he will come near to you.

When you know God's near you, When you know he's here, You know your room's filled with love._____ When you can re - mem - ber That God nev - er leaves you, You'll know your room's filled with love. God nev - er goes a - way from you. He pro - mised he'd al - ways stay. But you might for - get he's here, and then he'll seem so far a - way.

God nev - er leaves. He nev - er leaves.

He nev - er leaves. He's right there with you. That's

where he'll al - ways stay.

About the Author

Carol Smith, singer, songwriter, and producer, received her bachelor of arts degree from Bryan College, Dayton, Tennessee. She received a master of arts degree in religious education from Southwestern Seminary, Fort Worth, Texas. Since then Carol has served as a children's minister, Sunday school curriculum writer, director of Christian education, and contributor to several study Bibles. In addition to the piano and the guitar, she plays percussion and a little banjo, mandolin, dulcimer, and harmonica.

This book and companion tape have allowed Carol to focus on three areas that are important to her: children, music, and the Word of God. The music she has created will fill children's "drowsy minds and hearts with the comfort of God's truth as they drift off to sleep."

Carol now lives in Charlotte, North Carolina, where she is a full-time writer and musician.

About the Illustrator

Elena Kucharik, well-known Care Bears artist, received a bachelor of fine arts degree in commercial art at Kent State University. After graduation she worked as a greeting-card artist and art director at American Greetings Corporation in Cleveland, Ohio.

For the past twenty-five years Elena has been a freelance illustrator. During that time she was the lead artist and developer of Care Bears as well as a designer and illustrator for major corporations and publishers. For over eight years she has focused her talents in the area of children's book illustration, including all of the books in Tyndale's Little Blessings line.

Elena and her husband live in New Canaan, Connecticut, and have two grown daughters.